The
Cult Next Door

NATHAN COOPER

BOOK SPINE PUBLISHING LTD.

Table of Contents

The Arrival

Perspective 1: Sarah

The moving truck rumbled away, a gaping hole left on the pristine street. Sarah surveyed their new home, a charming colonial with a manicured lawn straight out of a magazine spread. Too perfect, a voice nagged at the back of her mind. But the exhaustion of the move battled with the flicker of unease. A fresh start, that's what she needed, what they all needed.

"This is it, kiddo!" Her husband, Tom, hoisted their sleepy five-year-old daughter from the car. Mia blinked, then let out a squeal, "A yard! A real yard!"

Sarah forced a smile. It had been years since they'd had space beyond a cramped balcony. Tom's job promotion was the unexpected windfall that allowed this move, a move away from the city, away from the ghosts that still lingered there. A bitter laugh threatened to escape. Briar Creek couldn't erase the screech of tires, the shattered glass, but maybe, just maybe, it could be a kind of balm. "Mrs. Carlson, is it?" A woman in crisp tennis whites beamed from the porch next door. Perfect teeth, perfect tan, she was a walking advertisement for the neighborhood. "Welcome! I'm Amelia, and I know you'll just adore Briar Creek."

Sarah felt Tom's muscles relax beside her. Amelia was his type – polished, cheerful, the kind that made him forget about spreadsheets and deadlines.

"Lovely to meet you, Amelia," Sarah returned the smile with practiced warmth. "The place looks just wonderful."
"It is!" Amelia chirped, eyes sparkling with an odd intensity that sent a prickle down Sarah's spine. "And wait till you see the fall foliage, it's breathtaking..." Her gaze drifted past Sarah to the street. "Ah! Here's the welcome committee!"

A gaggle of well-dressed women spilled from a gleaming minivan. Muffins and casseroles were thrust into their hands, followed by invitations to the book club, the garden society, the monthly potlucks. Sarah's fingers twitched for the cigarette she'd quit months ago. She craved the harsh bite of smoke against the relentless sweetness.

Perspective 2: Tom

A weight lifted off Tom's shoulders. It had been pure hell watching Sarah wither away in the city – the shadows under her eyes, the way she winced at sirens. The accident had hit them both hard, but while he buried himself in work, Sarah had withdrawn. This – the space, the smiles, the casserole onslaught – this felt like healing.

"Let's get everyone inside," he announced, his voice buoyed with an optimism he hadn't felt in months. "Mia, ready to claim your new princess castle?"

Her sleepy frown transformed into a grin. He scooped her up, delighting in the carefree giggle he hadn't heard in ages. Inside, the house surprised him. Bright, spacious, none of the cramped gloominess he'd expected from an older home. He caught Sarah's eye, saw a flicker of approval even amidst her weariness. Maybe, just maybe, things could be good again.

"Look, Daddy, a secret door!" Mia wriggled out of his grasp, disappearing into a tiny alcove under the stairs. He crouched down beside her. It was more a cupboard than a door, but the oddity sparked an unexpected memory. His aunt's creaky house, and that same mix of thrill and unease he felt as a child, exploring its hidden corners. A wave of nostalgia washed over him, tinged with something he couldn't name.

"Hey, can I help unpack?" Amelia's voice drifted from the kitchen, interrupting his thoughts.
"Sure, that would be grea..." He stopped dead. On the wall beside the cupboard, in the dim light, he swore he saw a symbol etched into the wood. Two triangles, interlocked. He blinked. It was gone. Just a trick of the eye.

Perspective 1: Sarah

The smiles never wavered. The offers of help were relentless. By late afternoon, Sarah felt simultaneously smothered and invisible. These women moved with practiced ease, their lives neatly arranged like those picture-perfect homes. She, with her rumpled clothes and city edginess, was the square peg they were determined to hammer into place.

Cracks in the Facade

Perspective 1: Sarah

The cracks appeared one by one, hairline fissures in the too-perfect facade. Mia's tear-streaked insistence on the "monster" wasn't a mere childish whim. Sarah now heard it too, the rhythmic thudding from above – measured, purposeful, the sound of something large and unsettling making itself home in their attic.

Tom dismissed it, but she caught his concerned glances when their daughter flinched at the sound, eyes wide with terror. One afternoon, while Tom worked inside, a flicker of movement in the backyard sent a chill down her spine. It was gone in an instant – a dark shape slipping behind the neighbor's toolshed like smoke dispersing. Had it been real? Or merely the manifestation of her mounting paranoia?

Briar Creek locals treated her with a mix of overly bright smiles and hushed whispers. In the checkout line, the cashier's gaze lingered a beat too long on her face before snapping away. "You're them, ain't ya? Moved into the old Henderson place. Best of luck to you then." The words were edged with a pity that curdled Sarah's blood. Best of luck? Just what exactly did that imply? The library offered a sanctuary, dusty and still, a world away from the relentless cheer of Briar Creek. While history books revealed nothing of note, the missing pet notices plastering the bulletin board confirmed her worst fear – Snowball wasn't an isolated incident. A missing tabby, a vanished golden retriever. The unease blossomed into full-blown dread.

Perspective 2: Tom

He was starting to hate the perfect lawns, the pristine houses, the relentless normalcy that felt like a stage set. It whispered of his failure – his inability to shield Sarah, to see even a flicker of joy reflected in Mia's eyes. Something shifted that week. Gone was Sarah's quiet withdrawal. In its place bloomed a simmering tension, a hunted look in her eyes that mirrored something in himself. It scared him, but also sparked a twisted relief. Sharing the burden didn't make the weight disappear, but it became a little less crushing.

One morning, an ominous silence greeted him in his makeshift office. Mia usually occupied a corner, her boisterous drawing sessions banished by Sarah until he finished work. He froze. The house was quiet – too quiet. Then, from the front porch, echoed Mia's panicked scream.

He found them huddled beside the mailbox – Sarah, pale as a ghost, clutching Mia, whose small body shook with sobs. On the sidewalk, scrawled in clumsy red paint, were two words: GO HOME

He swallowed hard. He'd failed to protect them again. That night, over a takeout dinner eaten in tense silence, a spark lit in Sarah's eyes. Not despair, but something steelier. Tom realized, with a mix of dread and exhilaration, they weren't running away anytime soon.

Perspective 1: Sarah

Enough. Sarah's hands curled into fists. Enough of the whispers, enough of the flinches, enough of feeling like a fragile trespasser in her own home. She craved the harsh, familiar bite of city streets, where danger was open, rather than this insidious, smiling threat.

The elderly librarian's words spun in her mind, the tremor in her voice a stark contrast to the cheerful ladies' club chatter. "Incidents… disappearances…" There was knowledge here, buried deep beneath decades of practiced, small-town oblivion. Someone in Briar Creek knew something, and Sarah intended to crack them wide open. The old Sarah, the one fueled by righteous anger, roared back to life. They'd picked the wrong woman to terrorize

The Cult's Invitation

Perspective 1: Tom

The scent of grilled burgers and the sounds of laughter pulled him out of his brooding. Amelia stood in their newly-planted flowerbed, waving enthusiastically. "It's the Founder's Day Picnic, Tom! You must bring the family!"

Her insistence overrode his hesitation, and the look of hope in Mia's eyes sealed the decision. An afternoon of normalcy, he told himself, that was all they needed. The Briar Creek park was transformed. Picnic blankets dotted the lawn, balloons hung from trees, and a makeshift stage held a grinning folk band. Sarah flinched at the noise, but Mia wriggled in delight, caught up in a whirlwind of face painting and bubbles. Tom forced a smile. It was progress, a glimmer of carefree joy he hadn't seen in ages.

Amelia appeared at his side, offering iced tea. "Enjoying yourself?" she asked, eyes twinkling.
"Very much," he replied, and he wasn't entirely lying. Amelia's relentless cheer was grating, and yet…it was hard not to be swept along by the infectious energy. The folks of Briar Creek were undeniably expert at throwing a party. The speeches began, a bland recounting of Briar Creek's founding fathers, a celebration of values any small town

would profess to uphold: family, community, tradition. It washed over him, white noise lulling him into a false sense of security. That was until the band quieted, and a man stepped onto the stage.

He wasn't young, but exuded an almost magnetic energy, radiating a warmth that drew the eye. When he spoke, his voice was smooth and hypnotic. He didn't preach, didn't spout ideology. He weaved simple tales of shared meals and helping hands, of belonging in a world that felt increasingly cold. Tom had heard a thousand motivational speakers, but this…this felt different. The speech ended on a crescendo of applause, and Tom found himself joining in, swept along by the collective euphoria.

Perspective 2: Sarah

Sarah kept to the edges, watching, analyzing. There was something…off. The practiced smiles, the overly intimate greetings, the way eyes lingered a second too long on her family. A group of women had surrounded Mia, cooing over her. Sarah itched to snatch her back and retreat, but Tom looked so… relaxed. It clawed at her, this desperate need for him to be happy, to feel like he wasn't failing them.

The man on the stage had a name, Edward. People spoke of him with a strange reverence bordering on worship. He was the architect of Briar Creek's unique "togetherness", a guiding light. She scoffed inwardly, her reporter instincts itching for a scoop. There was a cult hidden beneath this picture-perfect town, and she was damn well going to expose them.

As the sun began to dip, a hush fell over the crowd. Candles flickered, and hushed chanting drifted on the summer breeze. It was harmless enough, silly rhymes about friendship and shared harvest. For the first time, she saw a flicker of genuine emotion on the faces around her, something approaching religious fervor.

She turned to Tom. He wore a dazed, slightly awed expression. Her stomach sank. Had the siren song of community finally reached him too?

Perspective 1: Tom

It had been a good day, a genuinely good day. Mia's laughter was music he hadn't heard in far too long, and he could picture them fitting in here – cookouts, kids running in the park. The unease, ever-present, had softened around the edges. Maybe, just maybe, it was the fresh start they so desperately needed.

The after-party, under the twinkle of fairy lights, was where things shifted. The chanting stopped, but there was an undercurrent of energy, a focused intensity that sharpened the atmosphere. Conversations took on a hushed, conspiratorial tone.

There was an invitation, a chance to see Briar Creek's "true heart," a special gathering open only to the town's most dedicated members. Something about it pricked at him, brought back a flicker of unease. He looked over to where Sarah stood at the edge of the crowd, her face tight, closed off. The pull was undeniable.

To be included, to be part of the inner circle, to erase that look of distrust from Sarah's eyes… The temptation was a snake coiling around his thoughts. Yet, as he looked at their small family, a sliver of defiance ignited within him. His decision made, he squared his shoulders and walked over to his wife. They'd find their belonging, but it wouldn't be with the cult of Briar Creek

The Investigation

Perspective 1: Sarah

Sarah slipped into the library under cover of darkness. An unspoken alliance had formed with Mrs. Jenkins, the aging librarian. Armed with a weak smile and boxes of stale donuts, Sarah secured access to the musty backroom, the place where inconvenient truths were buried.

Old newspapers crackled as she scanned microfilm archives, searching for any mention of Briar Creek alongside words like 'disappearance', 'accident', or 'cult'. At first, nothing. Just decades of wholesome parades, piebaking contests, and overly enthusiastic obituaries.

Then, a pattern emerged. Brief, cryptic articles hidden away in the back pages, usually focused on individuals: loners, drifters, the kind who wouldn't be missed. A hiker vanishing on a trail, a homeless man found dead under dubious circumstances. The articles always ended the same way, a resigned acceptance, a case gone cold.

She followed the thread, a twisted breadcrumb trail spanning decades. Every few years, there it was, the hint of something rotten festering beneath Briar Creek's polished veneer. Fear slithered along her spine, but stronger still was the relentless pursuit of the truth, the burning desire to expose those who'd preyed on her family.

The internet offered less concrete evidence, but the pattern persisted. On obscure forums and local blog posts, she found whispers of unexplained lights in the woods, strange gatherings, and people who dared to question, only to vanish into thin air. The comments ended abruptly, the voices seemingly silenced. A fresh wave of terror rolled over her. Just how high did this cult's power reach?

Perspective 2: Tom

He was losing her. The distance grew each day, a gulf separating their small family. Sarah was consumed by what he was trying desperately to ignore. He'd caught her up late, hunched over her laptop, eyes wild with a manic energy that left him both terrified and deeply concerned.

One afternoon, he found her in Mia's room, sorting through old books and scribbling notes furiously. A prickle of fear ran down his spine. He recognized her focus, the same righteous fury that had carried her through her reporter days. They were over, those days. Or at least, they were supposed to be. "What are you doing?" he asked, his voice harsher than intended.

She whirled around, startled. Then, something seemed to crumble in her shoulders. Vulnerability crept into her voice. "Protecting our family, Tom. The way you refuse to."

The accusation hit him like a physical blow. The weight of it, the unfairness, almost pushed him over the edge. But he saw it wasn't malice, it was sheer terror fueled by love. With a sigh, he sat down beside her. "Show me," he said, "Show me what you've found."

She did. And with each news clipping, each cryptic forum post, he found a sliver of his complacency replaced with mounting dread. Maybe he'd been naive, perhaps willfully blind. He couldn't deny the evidence, nor the fire in his wife's eyes. The fight wasn't over, it was just beginning.

Perspective 1: Sarah

The dread settled in her bones with the certainty of an impending storm. They weren't dealing with some harmless community club. Decades of vanishings, hushed whispers... this was something organized, deeply rooted.

The cult had been operating with impunity for years, hiding behind the illusion of small-town charm. Then came the discovery that chilled her to the core. Deep in the archives, she unearthed an article celebrating Briar Creek's jubilee – 75 years of idyllic community life.

Yet the accompanying photo sent shivers through her. Edward, their charismatic leader, hadn't aged a day. Her breath hitched. How was that possible? The question lingered, a buzzing in her mind, the first hint of something far more sinister lurking beneath the surface.

The cult of Briar Creek wasn't just hiding secrets, it was defying all reason. She was in over her head, the dread deepening into a bone-shattering terror. And yet, she
couldn't stop. She had to find their weakness, strike before they swallowed her family whole.

The Inner Circle

Perspective 1: Mia

Mia loved their new house. Her room was big and pink, and best of all was the secret hiding place. Daddy had found it, a tiny space under the stairs where she could fit her dolls and all her most important treasures. But the best part was the special mark on the wall, the funny triangles that made her feel all warm and fuzzy inside.

Mommy wasn't happy about it. She said it was just an old mark and Mia shouldn't play down there. But Daddy smiled and said it was fine, and sometimes he even played with her in the hiding place. It was their secret. The grown-ups had been acting funny lately.

Mommy made hushed phone calls and looked worried all the time, while Daddy seemed… sad. That made Mia sad too. But then came the party, the one in the woods with bright lights and special songs the whole town knew. Edward said it was because Mia was so special, part of their big family now. She felt like a princess, and everyone was so nice to her! It made Mommy mad though. She scooped Mia away too fast, wouldn't let her play with the other kids. Mia just wanted everyone to be happy again.

Perspective 2: Tom

He was a fool. A blind, selfish fool for thinking they could find normalcy amongst the wolves. Sarah had warned him, her gaze filled with an accusation he couldn't quite face. Now, she barely spoke to him, her energy poured into endless phone calls, cryptic notes, and frantic trips to the library.

The pressure within their home was suffocating, a heavy silence broken only by Mia's chatter about the sing-alongs and the nice ladies who baked her cookies. Every time she parroted the cult's phrases, it felt like a tiny needle piercing his heart.

Then came the meeting - a "personal invitation" from Edward himself. Tom was ushered into a dimly lit room that reeked of incense and a sickly-sweetness that made his stomach churn. Edward, ageless and eerily calm, smiled at him.

"Your family, Tom, they could be truly happy here,"Edward crooned, his voice somehow echoing in the small space. "Belonging, purpose, peace… it's all within reach."

He spoke of Mia, of easing Sarah's anxieties, of providing a life Tom had failed to give them. His words weren't threats, but promises laden with unspoken consequences. It was a gilded cage, and they were the prey. A wave of nausea washed over him. He needed to get out, get his family and run, but Edward's gaze held him captive.

"Just give us a chance, Tom. Come to the Harvest Gathering, see the truth of Briar Creek for yourself."

Perspective 1: Sarah

She was failing. Failing to shield Mia from the insidious warmth the cult radiated, failing to convince Tom of the true danger, failing to crack the mystery that gripped Briar Creek like a noose. The phone call came late at night, a voice laced with pity, informing her that her old college roommate had vanished after moving to… of all places… Briar Creek. It was the final straw.

The threats were no longer subtle. Dead squirrels left on the porch – macabre warnings. Strange symbols scrawled on their fence, unseen eyes watching their every move. Briar Creek seemed to be tightening around them, threatening to suffocate them in its relentless kindness. Each morning, she'd wake expecting to find Mia gone, taken to be indoctrinated, turned into a smiling echo of the cult followers. The terror gnawed at her, twisting her into a creature she barely recognized. She was the hunted now, the prey trapped in a deceptively idyllic corner of the world.

Then, a glimmer of hope. A cryptic message slipped into her mailbox, promising information, a meeting point. Was it a trap? Most likely. But at this point, Sarah preferred certain danger to the endless, paralyzing fear. She was done hiding. It was time to fight back.

Perspective 2: Tom

Fear had sharpened his senses, making him see the cracks he'd willfully ignored before. There was the way Amelia would always appear right when his resolve wavered, the unsettlingly personal gifts left for Mia, the growing divide between himself and the wife he loved. He should have walked away when they first found the ominous warning painted on their sidewalk, but his desperation had overridden common sense.

The Harvest Gathering was his final chance, he toldhimself, a chance to see what the cult truly offered. It was almost laughable. Could sing-alongs and promises of 'belonging' truly combat the evidence Sarah had so painstakingly accumulated? He didn't know anymore. His logic was a flimsy shield against the despair gnawing at him.Sarah refused to go.

He understood, ven admired the stubborn defiance, but the fissure between them grew a little wider.

He was leaving her alone, venturing into the heart of danger, not to expose them, but because he desperately hoped they were wrong.

The Ritual

Perspective 1: Mia

The woods were magical at night. Mia skipped along beside Daddy, holding his hand tight, bright lanterns glowing against the inky darkness. It felt like an adventure, far more exciting than staying home with Mommy, who was always so serious these days.

The clearing was huge! It was filled with people in special robes singing songs from the party. In the very center, there was a big fire, and Edward stood really close to it, smiling just at Mia. It was time!

Daddy knelt beside her, his hand a little shaky. "Remember, honey, just watch Edward. You're going to be one of his helpers tonight." She felt so proud! Edward put a shiny crown made of
leaves on her head, and the whole crowd cheered. The man beside her, with the funny beard and twinkling eyes, whispered instructions.

It was scary at first, having to stand near the fire, but everyone was smiling and singing and that made it okay. Then, the man in the beard held out a basket, and something moved inside. It squeaked loudly! A tiny, furry thing, and she knew just what to do…

Her breath hitched. Not into the fire. She was supposed to lift the creature high, show it to Edward, and when he smiled, she was to place it into the… the box. The big, dark box with strange symbols painted on its sides.

Her throat felt tight, and the crowd seemed to blur. Daddy's voice was far away, "It's okay, sweetheart, just like we practiced." The lie hung heavy in the air. This wasn't a game, and those cries were full of terror.

Then, Edward's gaze held hers, his smile a twisted thing with no kindness behind it. She suddenly wished for Mommy, for her warm hugs and the way she could always make the bad things go away.

Perspective 2: Sarah

Her hands trembled as she dialed the number on the crumpled note. The voice on the other end was strained, barely above a whisper. "Meet me… old barn, north of the park… they know about you…" The line went dead. It was a flimsy thread, but her best, and possibly only, chance.

Dusk painted the sky in streaks of purple and orange as she crept towards the abandoned barn. Every creaking floorboard echoed like a gunshot. A dark figure materialized from the shadows, an older woman with eyes filled with a lifetime of regret and a flicker of defiance. "You have to get your family out. Tonight," the woman's voice rasped with urgency, "It's the Solstice

Gathering…they'll take her, like so many before…" She shoved a bundle into Sarah's hands. "Proof. Briar Creek ain't what it seems, and he…" she shuddered, "Edward… he ain't human…"

The words barely registered. Her child. Mia. "Where?" Sarah choked out, a mother's primal fear cutting through the confusion. "The woods…their sacred clearing…" The woman dissolved back into the shadows, leaving Sarah with only a bundle of old photographs that made her blood run cold.

Time blurred. Blind instinct propelled her forward, a desperate race against the setting sun. The photos showed decades of 'rituals', bonfires, and the same terrifying box etched with unholy symbols. She stumbled into the clearing just as the crowd erupted in a guttural chant thatseemed to shake the very earth.

And there was Mia, wearing a crown of thorns, her face tear-streaked and illuminated by the hellish fire…

Perspective 3: Tom

The weight of his deception crushed him. He'd brought them here, led his daughter straight into the heart of a nightmare. He barely registered the rhythmic chanting and the unsettling smiles, his gaze locked on two figures: Mia, her tiny frame swallowed by a ceremonial robe, and Sarah, her face contorted with a rage so terrifying, he almost turned and fled.

He'd wanted answers, something to ease the gnawing doubt. Now, he had them. The box, the terrified creature that Mia held aloft to the roar of the crowd, the flicker of something monstrous in Edward's eyes… it was a twisted mockery of faith, a perversion of his yearning for community.

Then, as if sensing his betrayal, Edward's gaze fixed on him. The chanting faltered, replaced by an anticipatory hum. He was no longer a guest; he was a sacrifice in waiting. Rough hands seized him, and in a haze of terror, he realized the gathering was only the beginning. He wouldn't be walking away tonight. And neither would Sarah, not if he had anything to say about it.

He saw Mia's mouth form a silent 'Daddy', eyes wide with fear, and a surge of adrenaline cut through the panic. The time for bargaining and appeasement was over. He lunged at his captors, roaring defiance. He wouldn't let his family be swallowed by this darkness without one hell of a fight.

The Escape Attempt

Perspective 1: Sarah

Her world had tilted on its axis. Fury and fear propelled her forward, a weaponized mother cutting through the crowd. Mia's scream tore through the chanting as Sarah reached her, snatching her daughter into a fierce embrace.

The memory of it all was a blur – shouts, hands clawing at her, Edward's face warped in monstrous rage. Then, Tom was there, a shield against the onslaught, his desperation mirroring her own. They ran, voices fading into the buzzing in her ears, Mia wailing against her. The woods were no longer a place of shadows but a maze of endless, suffocating darkness.

Finally, a flicker of light - the abandoned barn, and the woman, Mrs. Peterson, an unlikely ally with hands that shook as she pressed a pistol into Sarah's trembling grip. It wasn't safety, just a sliver of a chance before the hunters would descend. The hours blurred together. A stolen car, whispered arguments, and Mia's sobs. Tom was different, his despair replaced with a grim determination, a father willing to step into the darkness and fight for his family. It was a fragile unity, one born of terror and necessity rather than healing, but Sarah clung to it with a fierceness that surprised even herself.

The dawn brought with it the sickening certainty of pursuit. They couldn't outrun the cult, not for long. A sinking dread ate away at her, the whisper of a question she'd been avoiding: was this all for nothing?

Perspective 2: Tom

He should have listened. The guilt clawed at his gut. His desire for normalcy, for an easy fix, had nearly cost themeverything. Now, huddled beside Sarah in a stolen truck with their daughter curled catatonic between them, normalcy seemed an impossible luxury.

The road ahead was a blur. They were fugitives, hunted by a power they couldn't fully comprehend. Yet, seeing Sarah, the broken fury in her eyes mirrored in his own, gave him an unexpected strength. He had failed them enough.

His hand found Sarah's, a silent apology long overdue. She didn't flinch away, only squeezed tight. It wasn't forgiveness, not yet, but it was a start, a flicker of trust in the wreckage. They had to reach the city, Sarah insisted, get lost in the crowds, reach out to…she trailed off, the names of shadowy contacts from her reporter days mere ghosts of promises. It was a flimsy plan built on desperation.

He noticed her grip on the pistol tighten, her eyes forever scanning the rearview mirror. He swore to himself she wouldn't face the oncoming storm alone. His mind raced, 29searching for some buried survival instinct. Then, it struck: the fishing tackle in the truck bed. Hooks, fishing line…it was crude, but it could buy them time.

Perspective 3: Mia

Her world had shattered. The songs, the smiles, the warmth of the fire…they felt like lies burned into her mind. Edward, with the kind eyes, had turned into something else, a monster from her darkest nightmares.

Mommy and Daddy were different too. Their voices were tight, filled with words she didn't understand, and there was a darkness in their eyes that scared her almost more than the men with the strange robes.

The car rattled, bumping down unfamiliar roads. Mommy held her, her grip painful, a desperate attempt to keep her close. Daddy was in the front, looking out, holding the shiny thing Mr. Peterson had given them.

It was all wrong. She longed for home, even with the painted signs and the scary sounds in the attic. The woods, the bonfire…it had tainted everything.Her stomach churned, and a sob slipped past her lips. She just wanted it to stop, for everyone to be happy again, the way they were before… The thought snagged, an uncomfortable memory surfacing. The hidden space, the special marks, and the feeling they gave her. Had that been… wrong too? She couldn't tell anymore.

Perspective 2: Tom

The first sign wasn't a car chase, but the sickening absence of one. Silence where there should have been the relentless hum of pursuit. He voiced his fear to Sarah, who just nodded grimly, confirming his gut instinct – this wasn't a chase, it was a trap to lure them out.

They ditched the predictable highway for winding side roads, twisting through anonymous towns and desolate patches of countryside. Every mile was a gamble against the unknown, tension drawing the air taut within the car.

Then came the flat tire – not accidental, but carefully executed. As he changed the tire under Sarah's watchful guard, he realized their escape plan was a pathetic joke against an enemy with a decades-long head start. But he wouldn't give up, wouldn't let his daughter watch them all die.

He glanced down at the glinting fishing hooks – a cruel, desperate weapon, and the only tool he had left to fight the monster that was Briar Creek. Hope was a fragile thing, but for now, it fueled the fire in his gut. The hunted would become the hunter, if only for one bloody, desperate night.

The Confrontation

Perspective 1: Sarah

The barn loomed out of the fog, a rotting echo of the haven they'd barely escaped. This time, there would be no running, no hushed prayers for a miracle. This was where it ended, a blaze of desperate defiance against the encroaching darkness.

Tom moved with a chilling focus. Fishing wire strung taut between trees transformed the familiar surroundings into a deadly snare. Crude traps and makeshift weapons littered the ground. It wasn't much, but it was something, proof his pleas for action hadn't fallen on entirely deaf ears.

Mia, pale and withdrawn, sat huddled under a blanket, a terrifying echo of her former self. Guilt washed over Sarah. She'd dragged her daughter into this nightmare, and she would, by God, drag her out again. The first car appeared as dawn broke, a sleek SUV that whispered of power.

It wasn't the frantic mob Sarah had expected, but a calculated, chilling display of force. Four figures emerged, Edward leading them, his veneer of benevolence replaced with an unnerving calm. "Sarah," he called out, his voice carrying across the silent field, "It doesn't have to be this way. Mia belongs here, with us."

Each word was a lance of betrayal. "After what you did to her…" Sarah spat out, "She'll die before I let her go back to you!" "Such violence," Edward sighed, shaking his head, "We offer salvation, and all you bring is pain."

Then, just for an instant, a flicker of doubt crossed over his features, replaced quickly with determination. It was thecrack Sarah had been waiting for. He feared their defiance, their very existence outside of his control.

Perspective 2: Tom

The first cultist triggered his trap with a yelp of surprise. It was sloppy, clumsy, but it ignited a spark of feral hope within him. Their desperation was the cult's weakness. No rituals, no practiced chants, just an ugly brawl for survival. Tom, who'd cowered at office politics, found himself wielding a rusty pipe with terrifying efficiency.

Two against four was hardly fair, but Sarah fought besidehi with a ferocity he'd never witnessed. He saw her take a blow meant for him, the sight unlocking something primal within him. He wouldn't let her be the only casualty in the war he'd brought to their doorstep.

They were losing ground. Then, with a wail, Mia charged out from behind the barn. It was the last thing he expected – not a petrified child, but a girl filled with incandescent rage. She launched herself at Edward, a tiny, flailing body fueled by pure, defiant fury.

The moment of distraction was enough. Sarah seized the opportunity, lunging at Edward, the gun Mrs. Peterson had pressed into her hand a blur of motion. Edward staggered back, clutching his shoulder, and his followers froze in uncertainty.

The stalemate couldn't last. Tom knew it, and by the desperation in Sarah's eyes, she knew it too. It was time for one last, reckless gamble.

Perspective 3: Mia

The screaming was inside her head. It wanted to tear out of her throat, but she held it back. The bad man, Edward, he'd smiled at her but lied, like everything in Briar Creek was a lie. He hurt the creatures, and it was wrong. Their screams echoed her own terror in the firelight.

Her fingers fumbled with the heavy book Mrs. Peterson had hidden with the shiny gun. Pictures flickered past –scared people brought into the woods, the fire, the awful box with the marks she'd felt drawn to. A twisted coldness settled within her. They'd stolen parts of her, of Mommy and Daddy, and now she'd take everything back.The screaming swelled inside her. All the lies, the whispered manipulations, the smiles that hid fangs… they fueled a righteous fury. It erupted outward, a wail unlike anything she'd ever produced, echoing off the rotting barn, shattering the morning stillness.

The adults, locked in their battle, froze at the unearthly sound. For a heart-stopping moment, it felt like the world itself was holding its breath. Edward, clutching his bleeding shoulder, turned towards her, and she saw it – a flicker of genuine fear on his ageless face. The book in her hands didn't feel heavy anymore. It felt like power.

Perspective 2: Tom

The sound that erupted from his daughter was guttural, inhuman. It cut through the chaos of their struggle, silencing the shouts and the thudding blows. The cultists, so disciplined until this moment, recoiled, their controlled facade shattering.

Sarah reacted first. She surged forward, shoving the gun into Edward's chest with a snarl of pure hatred. "You'll leave her alone, you hear me? Leave all of us alone!" she spat, each word a testament to a mother pushed beyond all limits.

His followers hesitated, confused. Their leader, his facade of invincibility pierced by the gun and that bone-chilling cry, was finally vulnerable. It was the tipping point. Tom charged, knowing it was a gamble, but they'd gambled it all from the moment they'd moved to Briar Creek.

The men turned, not toward him, but toward their fleeing car. With a final, terrified glance over his shoulder at Mia, Edward followed. It was over, not with a dramatic victory, but a desperate, messy retreat born of a child's scream and a mother's love. Sarah slumped against him, sobs wracking her body.

Mia stood, still holding the worn photo album, her face drained of all color except for the fierce defiance blazing in her eyes. His heart ached for what she'd lost, for what they'd all lost. But in the wreckage, a flicker of twisted pride ignited. They'd survived.

The Aftermath

Perspective 1: Sarah

The hospital was a blur of sterile white and antiseptic smells, a far cry from the blood-soaked barn where they'd faced monsters. Each bandage, each wince of pain, was a grotesque reminder that the nightmare hadn't been a dream.

They'd survived, but they were far from whole. Tom lay pale and unconscious, a testament to the ferocity of their struggle. Mia sat hunched beside his bed, small and silent, her defiant light dimmed into a haunted flicker. Sarah's own injuries were a constant, throbbing ache, and beneath it all gnawed the suffocating guilt. She should have stopped this sooner, should have shielded them.

The police circled, cautious yet buzzing with the adrenaline of a major incident. Her statements, punctuated by Mia's raw recounts, fell into a chilling pattern: organized abduction, ritual sacrifice, decades of whispered coverups. Yet, the disbelief lingered in some officers' eyes, the same skepticism she'd once felt investigating the fringe conspiracy theories from her journalism days. Briar Creek had tainted everything.

The raid was swift, brutal, painting a picture of the cult's power. Underground tunnels, sacrificial chambers filled with grim remnants of those who hadn't been fortunate enough to escape. But Edward was gone, vanished like smoke. His followers, some captured, some killed in the confrontation, were tight-lipped. Their faith ran terrifyingly deep, leaving Sarah chilled. They'd cut the head off the snake, but it felt like they'd merely aggravated the body.

News vans descended, hungry faces and microphones demanding answers she didn't have. The town, once so idyllic, now throbbed with a mixture of fear and denial. Some looked at them with pity, others with veiled accusation. This was her fault, they seemed to say. She'd broken the perfect facade, brought unwelcome attention to the shadows lurking beneath Briar Creek's polished veneer.

Perspective 2: Tom

He awoke to pain and a sliver of sunlight cutting through the hospital blinds. Disorientation washed over him, then the memories came flooding back – the firelight, Mia's scream, the taste of blood and desperation. Sarah sat beside him, her face drawn and pale, but when she saw his eyes open, a flicker of relief sparked in her gaze.

The doctors spoke in hushed tones, a litany of cracked ribs and minor concussions. He'd heal, they said. But the deeper wounds, the unseen scars they all now bore, felt
more permanent. Mia hovered nearby, silent and withdrawn, and his heart ached for a childhood she'd lost
far too soon

Sarah relayed the news – the raid, the arrests, Edward's disappearance. Her voice was strained, carrying a weight beyond the physical toll. He reached for her hand, finally understanding the darkness he'd glimpsed in her eyes when they'd first arrived in Briar Creek. She'd been the watchdog, seeing what he couldn't, and the cost had nearly destroyed her.

He vowed then to make it up to them. They wouldn't stay. Briar Creek was tainted now, an open wound instead of a sanctuary. The question was where to go next. Could any town ever feel like home again, or would they be forever haunted by the cult next door?

Perspective 3: Mia

Her world was a kaleidoscope of shattered images. The warm smiles now had fangs. The sing-along songs echoed with the terrified cries of creatures she used to save. Even her beloved hiding place felt wrong, tainted by the mark of the box, a scar on her once happy home.

She wasn't the same. The happy-go-lucky Mia was locked away somewhere, replaced with a girl filled with cold rage and an unsettling emptiness. The book, with its yellowed pictures and tales of disappearances, had become a cherished weapon. She could feel the power within it, a testament to the victims of Briar Creek, a promise that what happened to her wouldn't happen again.

The hospital was full of whispers. Some said they were heroes, others seemed scared of them… especially of her. When she caught her reflection, she understood why.

Her eyes, usually sparkling with mischief, now held a darkness that mirrored the abyss she'd survived. She'd seen real monsters, and she wasn't sure the monster hadn't seeped into her as well.

Perspective 1: Sarah

The discharge papers felt like a cruel joke. Where did they go from here? The world beyond the hospital buzzed with an oblivious normalcy that churned her stomach. Their old life, the city apartment, the ghosts of their former selves, felt like walking backwards into an open grave. Briar Creek was broken, but it was all they knew.

Then, it came – a letter slipped into her mailbox during an errand, official letterhead bearing an address vaguely familiar. Mrs. Peterson's shaky handwriting covered a single page: an invitation to join a network, survivors of cults across the country, a shadow war hidden within the fabric of normal society. It was terrifying and absurd, and the only lifeline that felt remotely real.

Reporting the cult had been isolating. Now, there was a chilling sense of connection again. The world was wider, darker, and infinitely more complex than she'd imagined. The cult next door wasn't a local anomaly, but a symptom of a deeper rot, and they were now unwillingly inducted into the fight against it

The decision wasn't easy. It meant more danger, diving back into the very darkness they'd barely escaped. But as she glanced at Tom, at the haunted look in Mia's eyes, there was no real choice at all. They were survivors, scarred but unbowed. Briar Creek had been the battle; Sarah now saw a war looming on the horizon.

The Legacy

Perspective 1: Tom

The moving boxes felt heavier this time, weighted not just with possessions, but with the ghosts of what might have been. Briar Creek had shattered his illusions of safety, of simple fixes for life's complexities. He'd learned a brutal truth: darkness wasn't always visible, it could smile and offer cookies.

Sarah was a shadow of her former self, driven yet brittle. Late nights, she'd hunch over cryptic websites and old news clippings, tracing connections between Briar Creek and other small towns, other disappearances. It kept her focused, but at a price. He'd wake to find her still at the kitchen table, face pinched, eyes ringed with exhaustion.

They rarely discussed it. The unspoken fear festered between them, a heavy silence instead of comforting words.Mia was the biggest source of both hope and unbearable pain. She'd whip between clingy vulnerability and chilling bouts of icy rage. One day, it was tearful pleas to go back to their old house, the next, it was her meticulously drawing symbols from the photo album on the sidewalk with a ferocity that made neighbors cross the street nervously.

The new therapist spoke of trauma, of disrupted development. Tom hated the clinical words, but saw their truth reflected in his daughter. The carefree girl who'd chased butterflies was gone, replaced by someone older, wounded. His guilt was a constant companion.

Yet, he also saw glimmers of defiance. She'd guard thephoto album with obsessive intensity, whispering cryptic promises of "never again". The innocence was stripped away, but a warrior was emerging in its place. A dangerous path, he knew, but it was a fight he couldn't shield them from anymore.

Perspective 2: Sarah

The new town felt anonymous, comforting in its blandness. Yet, her gaze lingered on every overly friendly neighbor, every quaint store with its practiced smiles. Briar Creek had tainted her, stolen the easy trust she'd once taken for granted. Sleep was a luxury she rarely enjoyed. Nightmares plagued her – visions of flickering firelight, Mia's pleading screams, the chilling emptiness in Edward's eyes. Her reporter instincts raged, seeking patterns, connections, the proof that somewhere out there, the cult still pulsed like a dormant infection.The online forums had been a lifeline. Survivors like her, scarred but unbroken, shared fragmented whispers about similar towns, similar rituals. The scope of it all terrified

her. Briar Creek hadn't been an anomaly, but a node in a sprawling, sinister network.Her fingers traced the faded newspaper clippings she'd become obsessed with. Missing hiker, a 'tragic accident'; homeless deaths dismissed as a bad batch of drugs. Behind the carefully crafted narratives, she now saw the cult's hand, a legacy of calculated cruelty spanning decades, hiding in plain sight.

This wasn't just about survival anymore, it was about justice. It was finding every missing person, exposing every shadow, ensuring no other family would suffer what they had. The task was monumental, daunting, and it gave her the first true sense of purpose since the nightmare began.

Perspective 3: Mia

The box sat hidden under her bed. It called to her with a whispery promise of power, of control. She wasn't afraid of it anymore, not in the way she used to be. There was a darkness growing within her, fueled by a need for something she couldn't name. Justice? Revenge? It didn't matter, not as much as the satisfying burn of the rage coiling inside.

Sometimes, she'd hear the whispers from the box, faint and enticing. The marks on its surface pulsed with an unsettling warmth against her fingers. In the quiet of her room, she'd practice reading the faded words in the photo album, the chants and the rituals. It felt potent, dangerous… and it felt right.

Her parents looked at her strangely, a mix of fear and desperate hope. She didn't want their pity. She'd use the tools the cult gave her, twist their power against them. The thought sent a shiver of grim satisfaction through her.

One day, Edward would pay. They would all pay.She wasn't the only one changed. Her dad was harder now, a haunted look behind his eyes. And Mom… Mom was a warrior forged in fire, the righteous anger burningthrough her exhaustion. They belonged to the network now, whatever that meant, and she felt herself drawn into their orbit. It scared her, but the alternative, the hollow normalcy of her new classmates, was far more terrifying.

Perspective 2: Sarah

The news report was a blip on screen, easily missed. A fire at a remote compound, cult members dead or scattered. Then, the name flashed: Briar Creek.

But there was no mention of Edward, no image of his still form among the debris. Her finger stabbed at the rewind button, but the report moved on, insignificant to a world unaware of the true horror they'd narrowly escaped.

A wave of bitter triumph washed over her, quickly replaced by icy dread. It wasn't enough. It would never be enough until she knew Edward was gone, the ideology he embodied eradicated. The thought sent a tremor through her. Was that even possible? Had she become like them, consumed by an endless crusade?

A flicker of movement outside the window caught her eye. An ordinary car, parked across the street. After Briar Creek, nothing felt ordinary. She narrowed her eyes. Just a man, reading a newspaper. Or was he watching? Had they severed the snake's head, or merely angered the wider beast?

The doubt lingered as she made her way upstairs, a familiar weight settling in her chest. Mia was engrossed in the photo album, an unsettling intensity in her eyes. Sarah opened her mouth to intervene, but paused. The fight wasn't over. Neither of them were truly safe, and perhaps never would be again. But she saw the determination in her daughter's eyes, the echo of her own relentless fire. They were survivors, and maybe, just maybe, that would be their greatest legacy of all.

www.ingramcontent.com/pod-product-compliance
Lightning Source LLC
Chambersburg PA
CBHW060602100726
47907CB00005B/1477